Hate Mail

Hate Mail

Monique Polak

Orca currents

ORCA BOOK PUBLISHERS

Library and Archives Canada Cataloguing in Publication

Polak, Monique, author
Hate mail / Monique Polak.
(Orca currents)

Issued in print and electronic formats.
ISBN 978-1-4598-0776-1 (bound).—ISBN 978-1-4598-0775-4 (pbk.).—
ISBN 978-1-4598-0777-8 (pdf).—ISBN 978-1-4598-0778-5 (epub)

I. Title. II. Series: Orca currents
PS8631.O43H38 2014   jc813'.6   C2014-901563-1
                    C2014-901564-X

First published in the United States, 2014
Library of Congress Control Number: 2014935381

Summary: Jordie has a hard time going to school with his cousin with autism.

MIX
Paper from
responsible sources
FSC® C016245

*Orca Book Publishers is dedicated to preserving the environment and has
printed this book on Forest Stewardship Council® certified paper.*

Orca Book Publishers gratefully acknowledges the support for its
publishing programs provided by the following agencies: the Government
of Canada through the Canada Book Fund and the Canada Council for the Arts,
and the Province of British Columbia through the BC Arts Council
and the Book Publishing Tax Credit.

Cover photography by iStock
Author photo by Studio Iris Photography

ORCA BOOK PUBLISHERS
PO Box 5626, Stn. B
Victoria, BC Canada
V8R 6S4

ORCA BOOK PUBLISHERS
PO Box 468
Custer, WA USA
98240-0468

www.orcabook.com
Printed and bound in Canada.

17 16 15 14 • 4 3 2 1

*For my friend David Riverin,
who loves to read*

Chapter One

"Are we out of juice boxes?" I call out.

Mom walks into the kitchen. She's on the phone. I can tell from the way she keeps shaking her head she's upset. She must be talking to Aunt Anna. I bet they're talking about Todd.

Just before the school year started, Aunt Anna, Uncle Fred and my cousin Todd moved back to Montreal from a small town in upstate New York. We have more services for kids like Todd here, and Mom thought it would help Aunt Anna if they lived closer to us.

"Who would write something like that?" Mom says into the phone.

"Juice boxes?" I whisper.

She opens the cupboard under the sink, pulls out a packet of juice boxes and hands it to me.

"I hate orange," I mutter. But Mom isn't listening.

I toss a box of orange juice into my lunch bag. Maybe Tyrone will trade me.

Mom follows me to the front hallway. She tucks the phone between her ear and her shoulder so she can hear Aunt Anna while she kisses me goodbye. "Have a good day, Jordie," she calls out after me.

As Mom closes the door behind me, I can still hear her talking to Aunt Anna.

"What I don't understand is how anyone could be so deliberately cruel.

Not only to think those awful things, but to put them into a letter." There's a pause, and then she adds, "Thank goodness Todd doesn't know."

What letter? I wonder.

When I get to our locker, Tyrone is checking his cell phone—Tyrone is always playing with his phone. "What's good, bro?" he says, high-fiving me.

Samantha and Isobel walk by. They're both wearing tight striped T-shirts and short skirts. "Looking good, ladies!" Tyrone says, and they laugh. Samantha gives me a little wave.

I spot Todd coming down the hallway. I look away, pretending to search my locker.

The bell rings, and I slam the locker shut. The hallway is filling up with kids moving in every direction. Even if I wanted to, I couldn't see Todd now.

"Where's your babysitter?" I hear a guy call out.

I know without looking up that he must be talking to Todd. Correction: not talking to Todd. Talking at Todd. Except for the teachers and Darlene, Todd's aide, hardly anyone at school talks to Todd. Not even me.

"Aren't you a little old for a baby-sitter?" the same voice asks.

I don't hear Todd answer.

"Quit bugging him," a girl's voice says.

Then I hear a loud "*Oops!*" It's probably Todd.

When some kids start snickering, I know for sure it's him.

"Leave me alone!" He is shouting now. "Go away!" Up the hall, I see Todd is on his back on the floor, his arms flapping. Kids are backing away. When Todd loses his temper, he really loses it.

I feel bad for Todd, I swear I do. I know I should go over and help.

Except no one—not even Tyrone—knows that Todd is my cousin.

Where's Darlene anyhow? She gets paid to look after him.

As I'm thinking that, I spot the top of Darlene's head. Her curls make her look like a walking mop. "Todd! Are you hurt?" Darlene is one of those loud, slow talkers. It probably comes from spending her days shadowing kids like Todd.

I can't see Todd through the crowd of kids now, but I can hear his labored breathing as he picks himself up from the floor.

"Okay then," I hear Darlene say. "Up you go. It's a good thing you're not hurt. You're just a little dusty." She looks around at the kids still watching. "Did one of you push him?"

"I'm just a little dusty," I hear Todd say. If he was pushed, he doesn't tell Darlene.

I need to pass Todd and Darlene to get to history. I move as quickly as I can, elbowing my way past the other kids, hoping Todd won't notice me.

From the corner of my eye, I see the back of Todd's head. He has the same copper-colored hair as me. We got it from our moms. If I get too close to Todd, someone might figure out we are related. My life sure was less complicated before Todd turned up at my school.

Mr. Dartoni is at the whiteboard. "This morning," he says, "we're going to be looking at one of the most famous letters in Canadian history. It's a letter Louis Riel wrote to his followers. This letter was later used to convict Riel of treason."

It reminds me of the letter Mom and Aunt Anna were discussing on the phone. The cruel letter Todd is not supposed to know about.

Chapter Two

I try getting out of it. I tell Mom my English essay is due Tuesday and I haven't started yet.

Mom is pinching dead leaves off a houseplant. I can tell from the way she's concentrating—collecting leaf bits so they don't land on the carpet—that she isn't going to budge. "It's important to make time for family, Jordie," she says. "You'll write your essay tomorrow."

My dad is in the living room, reading the paper. "It'll be fun, bud," he adds without lifting his nose from the sports section.

It won't be fun, and we all know it.

We're going to the Pierre Elliott Trudeau Airport because Todd is obsessed with airplanes. Ask him how his day is going and Todd will start jabbering about wingspans, fuselage and vertical stabilizers.

It's part of Todd's condition, like going ballistic when he's angry and being unable to read other people's feelings. Most people can tell when someone's bored. A bored person yawns, looks out the window, checks the time. But even if you do all those things while Todd is talking about airplanes, he won't notice. He just keeps jabbering.

On our way to Aunt Anna's, I ask about the letter.

Mom and Dad exchange a look. "What letter?" Mom says.

"The one I heard you and Aunt Anna talking about. You used the word *cruel*. I figured it had something to do with Todd."

"I'd rather not discuss the letter," Mom says.

"Was it from school?"

"Jordie." Dad's voice is stern. "Your mother said she'd rather not discuss it."

Mom sighs. "And for god's sake, Jordie, please don't mention it in front of Todd. All I will tell you is that it's a disgusting letter—and it's about your cousin."

"You're kidding."

Dad sighs. "Why would your mother kid about something like that?"

Dad turns onto the street where Aunt Anna, Uncle Fred and Todd live.

Todd is pacing on the sidewalk outside the apartment.

"Be kind," Mom says.

"He's your cousin," Dad adds.

I slide open the back door of our van to let Todd in. "Hey, Todd."

It's as if he hasn't heard me. He doesn't say hi. He doesn't make eye contact. He just gets into the van, leaving this huge space between us. Then he starts bouncing in his seat. I get dizzy watching him bounce like that.

"Hi, Todd, honey," Mom says, flashing Todd a smile, which of course he doesn't notice. "How you doing?"

"We're going to the Pierre Elliot Trudeau Airport," Todd says. He's looking at his shoes.

As if we didn't know we were going to the airport!

Todd keeps bouncing. "The Dash 8 series was introduced in Canada in 1984."

The Dash 8 is Todd's favorite airplane. Thanks to our family visits to the airport, I'm getting to be kind of an expert in planes myself. "The Dash 8's the one with a twin engine, right?" I ask Todd.

"The Dash 8 is a twin engine turbo-prop," Todd says.

Mom pats Todd's hand. Just for a second, before he can object. Todd hates when people touch him, especially strangers. Mom is trying to help Todd work on that. "I hate to interrupt when you boys are bonding, but where's your mom and dad?" she asks.

Todd's bouncing again. "Inside."

Except for when he's babbling about airplanes, Todd uses really short sentences.

"I'll go get them," I offer. It's one way to get a break from Todd. He's not a bad kid, but, well, it's hard not being able to have a normal conversation.

I hear Aunt Anna and Uncle Fred coming downstairs. "I'll need to get footage in the arrivals area," Uncle Fred is saying. "Families meeting up after long absences. Guys holding bouquets and looking nervous."

"Can we discuss this later, Fred?" Aunt Anna sounds tired.

Uncle Fred jumps down the last two steps.

"Look who's here," he says when he sees me. "My favorite nephew."

"I'm your only nephew."

"Technicalities!" Uncle Fred ruffles my hair. "I was just telling your aunt about my idea for a documentary film."

A man walks into the lobby. He stops to look for something on the shelf near the mailboxes.

"Hi, George," Uncle Fred says to him.

George doesn't answer. He just mutters something about his newspaper. "That kid of yours didn't take it, did he?"

"Why would Todd take your news-paper?" Aunt Anna sounds annoyed.

"Well, I know he's got that…that…" George doesn't look at either Uncle Fred or Aunt Anna.

"Autism," Aunt Anna tells George. "Our son Todd has autism. I'm sure he didn't take your newspaper. In fact, I don't appreciate your making those kinds of remarks about Todd. You obviously don't know a thing about autism."

"We better go," I say quietly. I don't want Aunt Anna getting into a fight with this guy. Besides, Mom, Dad and Todd are waiting for us.

Uncle Fred doesn't seem to notice there's a problem. "Hey, George," he says, "when you have some time, I'd like to talk to you about this idea I have for a film…"

We park in the lot and then walk to the terminal. Mom and Aunt Anna are up ahead, followed by Dad and Uncle Fred. Uncle Fred is telling Dad about his idea.

Which leaves me with Todd.

I know I have to make an effort.
Todd is my cousin.

"Think we might see a Dash 8?" I ask
him.

"Do you mean the Bombardier Q400
turboprop?"

"I guess."

"The Dash 8 Bombardier Q400
turboprop arrives at 2:07 PM from
Radisson. The Dash 8 Bombardier Q400
turboprop was released in 2000. It has
the longest fuselage in the series."

"How do you know stuff like that?"

"Fuselage is the tube-shaped body of
the plane."

"You memorized that, right?"

"Uh-huh," Todd says to his shoes.

"You don't think that's a little
weird?"

"The Dash 8 Bombardier Q400
turboprop is more fuel efficient than the
Dash 8 Bombardier Q200."

At the observation area, I don't have to worry about what to say to Todd. All he wants to do is watch airplanes. He presses his face against the glass when a jet taxis in our direction.

"The Boeing 777 has the biggest tires on any commercial jet," he says when the plane comes to a stop.

I like planes too. But after twenty minutes of watching them and listening to Todd rattle off specs, I'm done.

Todd doesn't notice when I walk away.

Mom, Dad, Aunt Anna and Uncle Fred are sitting on benches, sipping coffee from paper cups. Uncle Fred is talking about his documentary. Aunt Anna rolls her eyes.

"Hey, bud," Dad says to me. "Having fun?"

"Sure," I lie.

Mom looks over to where Todd is. "You shouldn't leave your cousin alone like that."

So much for getting a break from Airplane Man.

I'm heading back to do my cousinly duty when I feel a light tap on my shoulder.

Before I even turn around, I know it's Samantha. No one else smells that good.

"Jordie!" she says. "What are you doing here?"

"I just came to watch airplanes with my—" I stop mid-sentence.

Samantha looks at me and then over to the window where Todd is standing, his face pressed against the glass.

"—with my parents. That's them over there." I point to the benches.

"Samantha!" a woman's voice calls from down the corridor.

"I better go," Samantha says. "We're picking up my grandmother."

"Well, good to see you…" It's not easy making conversation with a girl who smells as good as Samantha.

"Have fun," Samantha says.

I'm watching her walk away, when she turns around and adds, "With your parents."

Chapter Three

"Mind if we sit here, ladies?" Tyrone says to Isobel and Samantha.

Today's assembly must have been scheduled on short notice because there are no chairs out. The girls make room for us on the floor.

I'm sitting so close to Samantha our elbows touch. I owe it all to Tyrone. I might get better grades, but when it comes to talking to girls, Tyrone is at the top of the class.

There's static as Mr. Delisle, our principal, adjusts the microphone.

The teachers are seated on two long benches at either side of the gym. They make shushing sounds to signal the assembly is about to begin. Todd and Darlene are sitting on one of the benches too, but as long as I look straight at Mr. Delisle, they are out of my range of vision.

"Good morning," Mr. Delisle says. "I want to begin by saying a few words about bullying. It's a topic you've already heard a lot about, but I like to think I have something fresh to add to the discussion."

Some kids make shuffling noises at the back of the room, and somewhere closer to me, someone is whispering. Mr. Delisle waits until the room is quiet.

"As I'm sure you've all observed, each one of us is different. We come in different shapes and sizes. We like different flavors of ice cream. My personal favorite is double fudge."

A few kids laugh when he says that. "We all have different abilities, and we face different challenges," Mr. Delisle continues.

I think about how good Tyrone is at talking to girls and how terrible Todd is at talking to anybody.

Mr. Delisle clears his throat. "A lot of people speak about the need for tolerance. How we have to tolerate those who are different from us. But I don't think tolerance is enough—not for our community here at Riverview High School."

"I want you all to consider the word *tolerance* for a moment." Mr. Delisle pauses. I try thinking about the word, but I'm distracted by Samantha's smell and the feeling of her elbow against mine.

"We tolerate things we don't especially like. We tolerate rainy days and bruised apples. Don't tell my wife if you meet her, but I tolerate my mother-in-law."

This time, everyone laughs.

"This year at Riverview, we're not just going to tolerate each other. We're going to aim for something better. *Acceptance*." Mr. Delisle looks around the room, his gaze taking in each of us and stopping for the briefest moment in the far corner, where Todd and Darlene are.

He picks up a sheet of paper from the podium. "A few more announcements before you return to your classes. I know you're eager to hear about this year's class trips. The grade elevens are going to Quebec City. Grade tens will visit the Biodome and the Insectarium. The grade eights and nines are going to a flying school. And grade sevens, you'll be attending this year's Blue Metropolis Literary Festival."

There is some excited whispering after that, but Mr. Delisle isn't finished. "I nearly forgot to tell you—I'm implementing a new policy: Saturday-morning detentions. Students who are rude to their teachers, who skip classes, who miss their regular detentions or who engage in any kind of bullying behavior can expect to spend their Saturday mornings here with me in this gym. Now I want to wish all of you a pleasant day. I expect you to give serious thought to the matters we've discussed this morning."

The teachers stand up from the benches and wait for us at the back of the gym.

When I get up, I see that Darlene and Todd are still sitting. They must be waiting for the rest of us to leave.

Todd scratches under both his arms over and over. If a typical person's armpits get itchy, he might scratch once or twice. But Todd keeps scratching as the gym empties. When autistic kids engage in repetitive behaviors like that, it's called *stimming*.

"What's that freak doing?" Tyrone whispers. I know he means Todd.

"How the hell should I know?"

Samantha and Isobel are right behind us. "That doesn't sound very accepting," Samantha tells Tyrone.

Tyrone doesn't like admitting he's wrong. "Maybe the kid's got fleas." At least he didn't call Todd a freak. Tyrone turns to me. "Do you think he's got fleas?"

I pretend not to hear.

Tyrone nudges my shoulder a little too hard. "Do you?"

Samantha saves me from having to answer. She sidles up next to me. "Did I ever tell you," she says, "that your hair's a cool color?"

"Uh, no, you never told me. But, uh, thanks. It's nice getting a compliment from a girl…I mean from you." I realize how dumb that sounds. Why can't I be as smooth as Tyrone?

But Samantha doesn't seem to mind. She lifts her chin toward where Todd and Darlene are sitting. "You know what's funny? Your hair's the same color as Todd's."

The good feeling I got when Samantha paid me that compliment?

It's gone.

Chapter Four

"Can't we walk over?" I ask Mom. "You're always saying we should walk more."

Making kids attend parent-teacher night is another one of Mr. Delisle's bright ideas. At least tomorrow is a professional-development day, so we can sleep in.

"I know. But I told your Aunt Anna we'd pick her and Todd up."

"They won't mind. C'mon, Mom. When's the last time we went for a walk?"

"Okay," Mom says. "Let me phone and see if they can get there on their own."

The leaves have started to fall from the trees, and the air has a new crispness. Soon it will be Halloween.

"I forgot how fast you walk." Mom's cheeks are flushed from keeping up with me.

I can't tell Mom I am desperate to get to parent-teacher night before Todd and Aunt Anna show up. If anyone spots Todd and me with our moms, they'll know we're related. Mom and Aunt Anna look more alike than Todd and I do.

Mr. Delisle is waiting inside the entrance, shaking parents' hands.

Two grade eleven students are handing out a map of the school.

"Don't forget to check out the bake sale in the gym," one of them says.

Mom cranes her neck looking for Aunt Anna and Todd. I wonder if Mom has always felt responsible for Aunt Anna, who is four years younger than she is, or if she only started worrying about her after Todd got diagnosed.

I tug on the sleeve of Mom's leather jacket. "We should go right upstairs. That way, we won't have so long to wait."

There are already people milling outside Room 221. Mrs. Turcot, my homeroom teacher, has left the door open. She is sitting at her desk with a parent. A girl named Lisa, who's in my homeroom, hovers by the classroom door.

"Five minutes alone with the parent, then she invites the kid in. The whole thing takes ten minutes...unless of course you've got ADD or something," Lisa explains when my mom and I join

the line. "Don't forget the sign-up sheet."
She points to a sheet behind the door.

There are four names ahead of ours.
"Wanna sit?" I ask my mom. There's a
row of chairs in the hallway.

Mom checks the time on her cell.
"Maybe I'll go back downstairs and look
for Anna. Make sure everything's okay."

"No problem," I tell Mom. "I'll hold
our spot."

Tyrone hasn't turned up yet.
Samantha is not here either.

I take a seat in one of the chairs.
A group of parents are clustered nearby.
I'm not trying to listen in on their
conversation, but they're talking so
loud, it's hard not to.

"Who ever heard of Saturday-
morning detentions?" one mom says.

"I'm with you," a dad chimes in.
"It's ridiculous."

"You know what's even more ridiculous?" another woman asks. Her voice

is nasal. She lowers it before she goes on, but I can hear her. "Letting kids into this school who need all kinds of extra looking after."

I look up at the woman. She's got spiky blond hair, and she's wearing a black coat, with short black boots. "By the time kids get to high school, they should be able to manage without aides," she adds.

"And it's our tax dollars paying for those services!" a man mutters. "What worries me is that with so much money being spent on special-needs students, my kid won't get what he needs."

I know they're complaining about kids like Todd. If my mom were here, she'd say something.

I could say something.

Only I don't want anybody to know that Todd's my cousin.

By the time my mom gets back, our names are at the top of the list.

"Everything okay?" Mom asks. "You look a little off, Jordie."

"I'm fine. Did you find Aunt Anna?"

"Yup. I said we'd meet up with her and Todd later in the gym. At the bake sale. Someone mentioned chocolate cupcakes."

"Well, Jordie," Mrs. Turcot says when I sit down with her and Mom. Mrs. Turcot's mark book is open on her desk. "I've told your mom that overall you're a strong student. The only area that needs improvement is that sometimes you seem distracted."

"I'll try to work on that." I look Mrs. Turcot in the eye so she'll know I'm serious.

"My stomach feels kinda off," I tell Mom when our appointment is over. I put my hand on my belly. "I don't think a chocolate cupcake is a good idea right now."

"Do you feel like you're going to be sick?" Mom asks.

"Maybe."

Which is how I get out of going to the bake sale.

Mom gets Dad to pick us up. She makes him open all the windows in the van. She thinks the fresh air might make me feel better.

When we get home, Mom insists on holding my arm as I walk up the front stairs. I want her to think I'm still feeling queasy, so I stop on the third stair. Mom stops too.

Our eyes meet. I expect her to offer to make me tea or get me Pepto-Bismol. Instead, she gives me a sharp look and asks, "Jordie, have you told anyone at school that you and Todd are cousins?"

When I don't answer, Mom shakes her head. "There's something wrong with you, Jordie," she tells me, "and it's a lot worse than a stomachache."

Chapter Five

It's after ten when I wake up. The house is dead quiet.

I go down to the kitchen in just my boxers. If Mom were home, she'd make me put on a T-shirt. I leave the cereal box and my bowl, which still has milk in it, on the kitchen table. When I burp, I nearly apologize, but then I remember there's no one around to hear me.

Mom hasn't left a note. I turn on the TV, but there are only kids' shows and lame talk shows on. I should study for Mr. Dartoni's history quiz, but hey, I've got all day. I turn on the computer. I figure I'll message Tyrone, see what he's doing.

Maybe it's because I've got the quiz on my mind that my eyes land on the word *History* at the top of the screen.

When I click on *History*, I can tell right away Mom was the last one online. Who else would google spider plants and recipes for tofu teriyaki? I hope that isn't what we're having for supper. I scan the rest of the list. Mom's visited three websites about teens who have autism and a website about depression. The autism I get— Mom's trying to help Aunt Anna deal with Todd—but why is Mom looking up depression? We don't know anyone who's depressed, do we?

I'm about to click on the depression link when I notice the next item. It's Mom's Gmail account. I click on it.

A couple of seconds later, I am looking at Mom's inbox. I should tell her to make sure she logs out of her Gmail account when she's done. She doesn't want people reading her emails.

I should close this window, but I don't.

Instead, I scroll down the list of messages. She's got thousands. Hasn't Mom ever heard of Trash? Some of the messages are work related—people inquiring about Mom's houseplant watering service, her rates, whether there's a discount if they sign up for a year. But most of the messages are from Aunt Anna. They've got subject lines like *Having a really tough day, call me NOW!* and *Worried Sick About Fred*. Why is Aunt Anna worried about Uncle Fred? I'm about to click on that message when another one catches my eye. The subject line is only two words: *Hate Mail*.

I know even before I click on it that this must be the letter I heard Mom talking about on the phone. Most stuff you see on the Internet is typed out, so I'm expecting to see a typed-out letter.

What I don't expect to see is messy handwriting scrawled across a sheet of lined paper.

Aunt Anna must have scanned the letter. There's no date or greeting at the top; no *yours truly* at the end. It just starts.

I can't stand looking at that kid of yours. I'm sick of seeing him outside or in the schoolyard at Riverside, scratching under his arms and talking to himself like a lunatic.

Your kid's a freak.

I need to stop and take a breath after I read that. Sure, I think Todd is weird, and just last week Tyrone called him a freak. But seeing the word written out like that seems worse.

I don't know why you even let that kid out of the house.

You should keep him locked up so regular people don't have to look at him.

Or put him in a zoo where freaks like him belong.

The words are so mean, so angry, I can't keep reading.

I shut down the computer. My eyes are stinging. I turn the TV back on. A woman in heavy makeup is talking about a diet. "After a few days, you won't even miss sugar," she says, smiling into the camera. I hit the Power button on the remote to make her go away.

I go upstairs to get my history folder. It was wrong of me to open Mom's email. I should forget I ever saw that letter. Erase it from my mind the way

Mr. Dartoni erases the whiteboard at the end of class.

Except I can't.

The words I read keep coming back to me. *Your kid's a freak. Put him in a zoo where freaks like him belong.*

How could anyone think those things about Todd? I'm halfway up the stairs when I turn back. I re-open the computer and go back into Mom's email. The end of the letter is even worse than the beginning.

If you ask me, you should put that freak down, put him out of his misery. Just like you'd put down a sick animal. That freak of yours doesn't deserve to live.

I didn't really have a stomachache last night, but I've got one now. Even after I vomit into the toilet, my stomach still hurts.

Chapter Six

"I'm going to have to confiscate that gun," the security guard tells me.

"It's plastic," I tell him. "It's part of my costume. I'm a gangster."

But he insists. It's only when he's patting me down, checking for knives or alcohol, that I realize it's Mr. Delisle dressed up like a security guard.

"That's a very convincing costume, Mr. De—"

Mr. Delisle presses a finger to his lips. "What are you trying to do, blow my cover?"

I adjust my sleeves as I walk into the gym. I'm wearing my dad's black suit—Mom pinned up the pants, but the sleeves on the jacket are still too long—a black shirt and red tie. It's hard to believe this is the gym where we play basketball and floor hockey and have assemblies.

There are platforms for dancing and another one for the DJ. Paper skeletons hang from the ceiling, and there are jack-o'-lanterns on the table where a student council kid is selling soda and chips.

"I love your costume!" I hear some girl squeal. When I look to see who she's talking to, I know right away it's Tyrone. Who else would dress up like a rapper? He's wearing a velour tracksuit, with thick gold chains and a giant pair of headphones around his neck.

There are two girls with him. I can tell from her silver dress and pink hair that one is supposed to be a groupie. The other girl is wearing a black wig and a navy skirt and jacket. She must be some kind of businesswoman.

I make my way over. It's only when I get closer that I realize the girls are Isobel and Samantha.

Tyrone has one arm around Isobel's waist. I can't help feeling a little jealous when he wraps his other arm around Samantha.

"We're his dates," Isobel chirps. She even sounds like a groupie.

"You are? I didn't know we were supposed to have dates. How come you didn't tell me, Tyrone?"

Tyrone lets go of Samantha so he can smack the side of my head with the back of his hand. When he opens his mouth, I see the gold grill over his teeth. "It must've slipped my mind. But hey, you're welcome to hang with us. If the ladies don't mind."

"Of course we don't mind," Samantha says, which makes me feel better about the whole date thing.

"If you don't mind my asking," I say to Samantha, "what are you supposed to be?"

"Tyrone wanted us both to dress up as groupies, but I refused. I'm his producer."

"You look hot in that wig." Even before the words are out of my mouth, I realize how dumb they sound. "I mean you look...well, you know...good. Extremely good."

Samantha doesn't seem offended. "You look good too," she says. "Even if you're not really the gangster type. I like to think I'm the producer type."

"Totally," I say, which makes Samantha smile.

Tyrone and Isobel are first on the dance floor. When he presses up close against her, Mr. Dartoni, who is dressed like a priest, walks over and taps Tyrone's shoulder. "Not so close," he says.

I'm trying to figure out how to ask Samantha to dance. I don't think Tyrone asked Isobel; he just swept her onto the dance floor. I don't think I could do that with Samantha. *Do you want to dance?* Nah, too dorky. Plus, what if she says no?

I'm trying to come up with the right words when Samantha grabs my hand. "What are you doing?" I ask her.

"I was waiting for you to ask me to dance," she says. "But I ran out of patience."

The DJ is playing Eminem's "Same Song & Dance." Samantha sways to the beat. I nod when Eminem sings, "I like the way you move." Tyrone and Isobel are dancing next to us. Tyrone winks at me.

While we dance, Samantha and I comment on the other kids' costumes. "That's so original," she says about some guy dressed like a box of Chiclets. She also likes the girl in the mummy costume, her entire body wrapped in white medical gauze.

I don't think anything about it when a guy in a pilot's uniform passes the platform where we're dancing. I only see the back of him: shiny black cap, white shirt with gold epaulets, gray pants.

Samantha nudges me. "I don't see Kool-Aid. Do you?"

"I don't see Kool-Aid either, just 7-Up and Coke. You thirsty? You want to get something to drink?"

"I said, 'I don't see his aide.'" Samantha shouts so I can hear her over the music. She lifts her eyes in the pilot's direction. How could I not have known it was Todd? Then again, I didn't expect him to show up at a school dance.

"His aide must be here somewhere. His parents wouldn't let him come to a dance unsupervised. They'd have hired Darl—" I stop myself. I don't want to sound like I know too much about Todd.

"Oh, there she is!" Samantha says. Now I see Darlene too. She's in line at the refreshments table. She's dressed as a unicorn, with her horn wrapped in tin foil. Maybe it's her way of saying it's good to be different.

I don't know where Todd is. The lighting is dim, making it hard to see. Why am I worrying about him anyway? That's Darlene's job.

A guy from homeroom is dressed like a hockey puck. "That's a cool costume," I say to Samantha, but her back is turned to me now, and she's dancing with Isobel.

I don't understand girls.

Since I'm not one of those people who enjoys dancing alone, I step off the platform, hoping no one is watching me.

I'd buy a soda, but I don't want to get stuck talking to Darlene—or Todd.

I go stand by the wall. Isobel and Samantha are still dancing. I wonder where Tyrone is. When I get tired of standing around, I take a bathroom break.

Even before I walk into the bathroom, I can hear laughter. What's going on in there?

Tyrone is sitting on a chair blocking one of the stalls. He moves his head to the beat of the music he is listening to.

The laughter comes from Mark, one of Tyrone's buddies, who is wearing a Spider-Man costume. "If you were a real rapper," Mark tells Tyrone, "you wouldn't be listening to music in some bathroom. I'm getting outta here. Why don't you just leave whoever's inside there alone? I'll wait for you outside."

That's when I realize someone is trapped inside the stall.

Whoever it is has started banging like crazy on the stall door.

Tyrone has this big dumb smile on his face.

The guy inside bangs harder. He's going to hurt himself if he keeps that up.

It's not nice to tease some kid the way Tyrone is doing, but I have to admit it's kind of funny to hear the guy freaking out.

Now he's trying to crawl out from underneath the stall door.

Tyrone laughs as he swats at the guy's hands.

The guy starts howling. It's this weird high-pitched nervous howl. Only one person howls like that.

Todd.

"Let him out!" I tell Tyrone.

Mark bangs on the bathroom door then pushes it open. "Security's coming!" he hisses.

Tyrone pulls the chair out of the way. "Okay," he says, "whoever you are, joke's over. You can come out now." But Todd is howling so loud he can't hear Tyrone.

If Todd knew I was here, it might help him calm down. But there's no way I want Tyrone to know Todd and I are related.

Mr. Delisle bursts into the bathroom. Todd is still blubbering. He won't come out of the stall. I see Mr. Delisle's eyes land on the chair behind Tyrone. I know he's piecing together what has happened.

Darlene is outside, shouting, "Are you in there, Todd? Todd, are you all right?"

Mr. Delisle walks over to the stall door. "Todd," he says, "it's me, Mr. Delisle. I'm sorry for what's happened.

47

I'm going to ask the others to leave. When you're ready, you can come out. Darlene is waiting for you outside the bathroom. Are you okay with that, Todd?"

The blubbering lets up and Todd says, "Okay."

Mr. Delisle curls his finger to indicate he wants to talk to me and Tyrone outside. We follow him to the corridor. Mr. Delisle's dark eyes look even darker than usual.

"It was just a joke. I swear I wouldn't have done it if I'd known it was him inside," Tyrone tries telling Mr. Delisle.

"I had nothing to do with it," I add. "I just walked in and…"

Mr. Delisle waves the back of his hand in the air as if Tyrone and I are mosquitoes he would like to swat.

Mark is running down the hall with Isobel and Samantha. Mr. Delisle calls them over. "Saturday-morning detentions," he says in a voice I've never heard him use before, "for every one of you!"

"We didn't do anything," Isobel says. "We were just talking to Mark."

"I'll see all of you at eight AM sharp on Saturday," Mr. Delisle says.

Then Mr. Delisle turns to Darlene. "I'll need to speak with you and Todd later. But you can let him know he's got a detention too—for not telling you he was leaving the gym."

"You can't go giving out detentions like that," Mark says. "You're a security guard!"

Tyrone nudges Mark. "That's no security guard, doofus," he says. "That's Mr. Delisle."

Chapter Seven

When I see the lights on in the living room, I think my parents must be watching late-night TV.

But the TV isn't on. Dad is in his armchair. Mom is on the couch across from him. They're speaking in low voices, but the conversation stops when I walk in. That's how I know they're waiting for me.

Do they know about the detention?

"Did you have fun?" Mom asks.

"Dance with any good-looking girls?" Dad wants to know.

"Yes and yes." I'm thinking that if they heard about the detention, they would have mentioned it. "It's pretty late. I better get to bed."

Mom uncrosses her legs. "We wanted to have a word with you."

"Now?"

Mom nods. She looks so serious that for a moment I think they do know about the detention.

"It wasn't my fault."

"What are you talking about, Jordie?" Dad asks.

I need to change the subject—fast. "What exactly do you want to talk to me about?" I don't sit down. That way I might still be able to get away.

Dad must know what I'm thinking. He gestures toward the empty spot on the couch. "Have a seat."

I plop down. Mom moves in a little closer. "We want to talk to you about your cousin. About Todd."

"I know his name."

"Jordie, don't be rude to your mom."

"Sorry, Mom." I don't look at her when I apologize.

"We know it isn't easy for you." Dad doesn't say what *it* is, but I figure he means having Todd for a cousin.

"When I was your age," Mom adds, "all I cared about was wearing the same brand of jeans as the other girls."

"What do girls' jeans have to do with anything?" I ask.

I half expect Dad to tell me I'm being rude again, but he doesn't. "What your mom means is that when you're a teenager, you put a lot of stock in what other kids think of you. Too much stock."

"You can't keep hiding the fact that you and Todd are related." Mom sighs after she's said that. Dad sighs too.

"Having a cousin who's a fr—" I stop myself. But I can tell Mom and Dad know what I was about to say. "—who's autistic is a lot harder than not having the right pair of jeans."

"It's a lot harder for Todd than it is for you," Mom snaps.

I try to explain. "I guess I worry if the other kids know Todd and I are related, they'll look at me differently. They'll laugh at me."

"Laugh at you? For having a cousin who has autism? Why, that's ridiculous!" Mom says.

"I think we need to go at this from another angle," Dad says. "Todd needs your support. He looks up to you, Jordie. He's proud to be your cousin."

"Proud? Proud's a feeling. Todd doesn't have feelings!" I don't mean to raise my voice.

"Jordie, we've been over this a hundred times. Of course Todd has feelings,"

Mom says. "It's just hard for people with autism to express their feelings."

"Look, I don't know why we've got to have this conversation right now." I get up from the couch and start heading upstairs.

"Your Aunt Anna's having a hard time," Dad says to my back.

I turn to look at him and Mom. "Is that supposed to be some kind of news-flash? I know Aunt Anna's having a hard time. Mom spends half of every friggin' day on the phone with Aunt Anna talking about it." I'm raising my voice again.

"It isn't only Todd she's worried about…" Mom says quietly.

I'm only half listening. Maybe because I'm too ticked off. It's only when I'm putting on my pajamas that I think about what Mom just said. By then, Mom and Dad are upstairs too. I hear them in the bathroom, brushing their teeth.

I open my bedroom door and call out, "What else is Aunt Anna worried about?"

The brushing sounds stop and then Dad says, "Maybe it's better if we talk about it in the morning."

I need to brush my teeth too. They're both still there when I get to the bathroom. Mom's putting on face cream. Dad's flossing.

"So what's wrong with Aunt Anna?"

Mom and Dad exchange a look in the mirror.

"It's Uncle Fred," Mom says.

"He's depressed," Dad adds.

"Uncle Fred—depressed? What are you talking about? He was in a great mood when we went to the airport."

Mom and Dad exchange another look. They're deciding how much to tell me.

Mom replaces the lid on her jar of cream. "When we went to the airport, he was in one of his up phases. Now he's in a down phase."

"Everyone has ups and downs," I say.

Mom sighs. "What your Uncle Fred has is different. We're pretty sure he has something called manic depression. He's had it before."

"He has? How come I never heard about it?"

"You were little the last time it happened," Mom says. "It was just after Todd was diagnosed."

I don't say what I'm thinking—that if I was a dad and my kid got diagnosed with autism, I'd be depressed too.

Chapter Eight

If Mom and Dad sleep in, I should be able to slip out to Saturday-morning detention without telling them about it. Or at least without telling them about it in person. They'll need to sign a form, but I'll worry about that later.

I tiptoe downstairs and try not to crunch when I eat my cereal. Because I know they'll wonder where I've gone, I leave a note on the kitchen table.

Dear Mom and Dad,

Since you were already kind of upset last night, I didn't think it was a good time to tell you I got a Saturday morning detention. Honestly, I didn't do anything wrong. It was a case of being in the wrong place at the wrong time. Detention's over at 12:30. I'll come straight home. Your son, Jordie.

I'm crossing out the *Your son* part (they know I'm their son) when the phone rings. I spring up from my stool to grab the portable, but the damage is done. Mom has picked up the phone in her bedroom. "Anna," I hear Mom say, her voice still groggy, "is it Todd? Or Fred?"

I put my bowl in the dishwasher and grab my jacket.

I slip out the front door and take a deep breath. That was a close call.

Better that I'm not around when Mom finds out about the detention.

I break into a jog. Moving feels good. I'm not looking forward to spending four and a half hours staring at the gym walls, but at least Samantha will be there.

I hardly notice when a van pulls up at the Stop sign. Not until the passenger window rolls down, and I see my mom behind the wheel. In her penguin pajamas! I turn around to make sure no one's watching.

"Mom, you can't drive around in your pajamas!"

"Get in the van, Jordie!" I can tell from her voice she means business.

"I think it's better if I walk. I can use the exercise. Look, I'm sorry I didn't tell you about the detention."

"That's not all you didn't tell me about, Jordie. In the van! Now!" I get in.

"Why didn't you tell me Todd got a detention too?"

"I figured you'd find out. Are you planning to drop me off at school? Maybe you could leave me at the corner. No offense, but I don't want anyone knowing my mom drives around town in penguin pajamas."

I think maybe that will make Mom laugh, but it has the opposite effect. "You know what your problem is, Jordie? You care way too much about what other people think!"

I don't say anything after that, and neither does Mom. She drives right up to the front entrance. Tyrone is coming from the other direction. I try not to care when he walks up to my mom's door. "Good morning," he says. "Nice pj's!"

I'm getting out of the van when my mom puts her hand on my elbow. "Jordie, like it or not, you're going to have to keep an eye on your cousin today."

I turn around to face her. "What about Darlene?"

"Mr. Delisle asked Darlene to come in, but she wasn't available. He couldn't find a replacement. So you're it." There's no point in arguing.

There's a row of desks at the front of the gym. Samantha, Isobel and Mark are already there.

Mr. Delisle comes in after us. He is wearing a plaid shirt and jeans. Seeing him dressed like that is almost as weird as seeing him in a security guard costume. "Have any of you seen Todd?" he asks. "What about you, Jordie?"

"Nope, I haven't seen him." I try to keep my voice casual. I'm willing Mr. Delisle not to tell the others that Todd is my cousin.

Mr. Delisle gives me an odd look. "Well then, Jordie," he says, "could you wait by the front entrance and bring Todd to the gym once he arrives?"

When I get to the front entrance, Aunt Anna is there, helping Todd take off his coat. She waves when she sees me. "You'll look out for him, won't you, Jordie?" she asks me.

"Uh-huh," I tell her. "Okay, Todd." I gesture for him to follow me. I know he'll get upset if I take his arm. "We're going to the gym."

Todd's eyes are fixed on the floor. "I got a detention," he says. "I didn't tell Darlene I was going to the bathroom. And then the door wouldn't open. That made me mad."

"You won't let anyone tease him, will you?" Aunt Anna whispers to me.

I follow Todd down the hallway. What would it be like, I wonder, to have a normal cousin? Someone to hang out with, play video games, listen to music, talk about girls. Sometimes, it sucks to be me.

When we get to the gym, the others aren't at their desks. They are by the bleachers, huddled around Mr. Delisle.

Mr. Delisle waves when we come in. "Over here!" he calls out.

I go stand between Tyrone and Samantha. Todd stays a few feet back from the rest of us.

"I don't see much point in having you people sit around twiddling your thumbs for four and a half hours," Mr. Delisle says. "I'm sure you'd prefer to do something useful. So you're going to spend the morning cleaning up the schoolyard."

"Isn't child labor illegal?" Tyrone asks.

"Nothing illegal about it," Mr. Delisle tells Tyrone. "Not if the tasks contribute to youngsters' education, health, physical and moral development. And I promise you—they will." Why am I not surprised he knows all about child labor laws?

"I wish you'd told us we'd be working outside," Isobel says to Mr. Delisle. "I wouldn't have worn a skirt."

Chapter Nine

I have to give Mr. Delisle credit. He could make us do all the work, but he's raking leaves too. His face is shiny with sweat. The seven of us are stuffing leaves into giant compostable paper bags. The wind is blustery, and we have to hold on to the paper bags so they don't fly away. I pull my tuque down over my forehead.

Mark hasn't got a hat. He looks different without gel in his hair. "Isn't this the janitor's job?" he grumbles.

Mr. Delisle leans on his rake. "You complaining, Mark?"

"No, sir. Just asking."

"Hey, there's a leaf in your hair," Tyrone tells Isobel. He pulls the leaf out and hands it to her. Isobel giggles. Only Tyrone could find a way to turn detention into a way to impress girls.

Todd isn't saying anything, which is better, I guess, than babbling about Dash 8s. He isn't working as quickly as the rest of us. Maybe it's because every time he scoops another bunch of leaves into his bag, he tamps them down.

"Hey, Mr. D, if we get these leaves cleaned up before twelve thirty, you gonna let us go home early?" Tyrone asks.

Mr. Delisle puts down his rake and uses both hands to massage his lower back. "Did I mention the leaves in the side yard? There are twice as many there as there are here."

Tyrone groans.

"Do you think I can leave the six of you to your own devices for a few minutes?" Mr. Delisle asks. "I need to go inside and get some aspirin."

"We'll be fine," Tyrone answers for all of us.

"Good," Mr. Delisle says, "because I'd hate to have to give you all another Saturday detention. Mind you, the boiler room could use a scrub."

Once Mr. Delisle is out of sight, Mark and Tyrone stop scooping leaves. Tyrone pulls his cell out of his pocket and checks for new messages. Mark is watching Todd. "Hey, buddy," he tells him, "it'd go a lot faster if you waited to do that till your bag was full."

Mark's tone is friendly, but Todd isn't any better at recognizing a person's tone than he is at reading body language. He doesn't say anything.

"Did you hear me?" This time, Mark's tone is less friendly.

Todd still doesn't respond.

"Well, did you?"

"Uh-huh," Todd finally answers. Only he's still tamping down the leaves.

I think about the promise I made to my mom and Aunt Anna. I take a deep breath. "Maybe you should leave Todd alone," I tell Mark. "We've all got our own way of doing stuff. Doing things in a certain order makes him feel better."

Samantha, who is crouched on the ground near me, gives me a smile. The cool air has made her cheeks red.

Mark lifts his chin in my direction. "What are you? Some kind of expert on freaks?"

My heart is thumping in my chest. I know Samantha is listening, and that makes me want to do the right thing.

"Todd's not a freak. He has autism. Lots of people have it." I know this would be a perfect moment to say that Todd's my cousin, but I don't.

I can't.

Just then, the back door of the school swings open and Mr. Delisle comes out. Mark and Tyrone start shoveling leaves into their bags again.

"It's recess time," Mr. Delisle call out. "I brought you a little snack."

"He's not a bad guy," Isobel says, "for a principal."

Mr. Delisle has granola bars. They're not the store-bought kind we're used to. "My wife made them," he explains, handing them out. "They're wheat-free. She wants me to cut back on gluten."

Mr. Delisle doesn't rake as quickly as he did before. I catch Mark looking over Todd's shoulder a couple of times. I don't understand why it bugs Mark so much that Todd keeps tamping down the leaves in his bag. I'd say something, but I'm afraid Mark will start ragging on me again.

I'm lugging bags to the compost bin when I notice Mark hunched over Todd. Now what's going on?

I rush over. Mark is showing Todd how to fill his bag more quickly. "Like this," he's saying as he shoves leaves into the bag.

Mr. Delisle has come over too. "Leave Todd alone," he tells Mark.

"I'm just trying to help him." Mark claps Todd's back. Mark doesn't know Todd hates to be touched.

It is a simple gesture—Mark meant to show he didn't mean any harm—but it sets Todd off.

"Don't touch me!" Todd wails so loudly that if anyone in the neighborhood is trying to sleep in, they are awake now.

Mark backs away, but Todd keeps wailing. "Don't touch me! I told you not to touch me! Stop! I said stop!"

Only, the person who can't stop is Todd.

"Let's give Todd some space," Mr. Delisle says. He looks worried. He's used to having Darlene around to help with Todd. Mr. Delisle drops his voice. "Everything's going to be okay, son," he tells Todd.

Samantha is next to me. "Aren't you going to help?" she asks.

I go over to Todd. I don't touch him. I try talking the way I've heard Aunt Anna and Mom talk to him—in a low, soothing voice.

"It's me—Jordie." I'm talking so quietly I'm sure the others can't hear me. "I'm here. No one's going to hurt you, Todd."

Mr. Delisle has stepped away to give us some privacy. "The rest of you," I hear him tell the others, "back to work."

It takes Todd a while to settle down, but he does.

When I'm back to stuffing leaves into a bag, Mark nudges me. "I didn't know you were so good with freaks," he whispers.

"Quit calling him a freak!" I whisper back.

Samantha is close enough to overhear our conversation. I smile at her, expecting her to smile back. She must be impressed I stood up for Todd.

But she just shakes her head.

"Is something wrong?" I ask her.

Samantha shakes her head again. "I don't know why you can't admit you two are related."

Chapter Ten

I'm not the kind of kid who listens in on other people's phone conversations.

What happens is I'm in the kitchen, about to call Tyrone, when I pick up the portable and hear Mom and Aunt Anna talking.

I could say "Oops" and hang up, but, well, I don't.

They are discussing the letter. Aunt Anna doesn't use the word *letter* though. She uses the words *hate mail*.

"The police say it's a hate crime, but that there isn't much they can do about it. That's why I'm going public. You can't keep telling me not to, Julie. I've had it with pretending everything's okay. There are horrible people out there, people who hate kids like my son. I want to expose that hatred." Aunt Anna is sobbing.

"Oh, Anna," Mom says and I can practically see her wringing her hands, "I know how hard this is for you. But you need to think about Todd—about what's best for him. He's a shy child. If you go to the media, there will be interviews."

I'm picturing it in my head, Todd's face in the newspaper and on TV, his voice on the radio. It would be a total disaster! And what if people see Aunt Anna and they figure out she's mom's sister and I'm Todd's cousin? Then what?

"They won't want to talk to only you, Anna," Mom continues. "They'll want to talk to Todd. And what if he finds out about what's in the letter? Frankly, I don't think he could handle it." Mom pauses. "Even a normal child would find it difficult."

Yikes, I think to myself, that's the worst possible thing to say to Aunt Anna.

"*A normal child*? My god, Julie! I can't believe you just said that! How many times have I told you children with autism are not *abnormal*?" I'm surprised at how quickly Aunt Anna switches from sad to angry.

"I'm so sorry, Anna. Of course, I know you're right. The word just slipped out, I think because I'm so ups—"

Aunt Anna won't let her finish. "I know you try to be a good sister and a good aunt, but sometimes I think you don't understand what my life is like!

75

Between looking after Todd and worrying about Fred!"

"I'm trying to understand, Anna, honestly I am. I know how tough things are. I'm trying to be supportive. Why do you think I encouraged you to move back here? But maybe with so much pressure…you're not thinking clearly."

Aunt Anna makes a noise that sounds like a growl. "For your information, I am thinking perfectly clearly. And let me tell you something else: just because you're my big sister doesn't mean you're always right. You always try to smooth things over, but you know what, Julie? Sometimes it's better to stand up. Even if it's hard!"

When Aunt Anna says that, I remember what happened at detention. I tried standing up for Todd, and Aunt Anna is right, it was hard.

Mom won't back down. "This isn't about you, Anna. It's about Todd and what's best for him. I know you're upset, but you have to put your son first."

"Don't speak to me like that," Aunt Anna hisses. "I have always put Todd first. Always. You know that!"

"Anna, can you at least agree not to do anything rash? Can we talk about this in a few days when we've both calmed down?"

"All right," Aunt Anna says, "I'll wait a few days. But I'm warning you, Julie, if I still feel like this, I'm going ahead with my plan."

Mom sighs into the phone. "I think a few days will give you some perspective. By the way, have you talked to Fred about it?"

"Fred?" Aunt Anna laughs. It's not a happy laugh. It's an I-can't-take-much-more kind of laugh.

"Yes," Mom says, "how does Fred feel about your plan to go public with the letter?"

"Fred?" Aunt Anna says again. I wonder if maybe Aunt Anna is cracking up too. "Fred can't talk about anything except that ridiculous movie he wants to make. He hasn't slept in two weeks. He's up writing treatments and proposals."

"Oh no." Mom sounds almost as distressed as when Aunt Anna was talking about the hate letter.

Neither of them says anything for a moment. Then Mom adds, "The not sleeping. Isn't that what happened last time?" Mom pauses. "Before he crashed?"

Chapter Eleven

Mom is usually out watering plants when I get home from school Tuesdays. So when I see the van in the driveway and Mom in the front window with her jacket on, I know something's wrong.

"I need your help," she says when I come in.

"What for?"

"We've got to get right over to Anna's. It's an emergency."

"Have you ever noticed," I say, when we're in the van, "how it's always an emergency with Aunt Anna?"

Mom doesn't stop for a yellow light. "You know what I've noticed, Jordie?" she says. "That you're only interested in your own well-being."

"Ouch," I say. "That hurt."

But is it true?

When we reach the third floor where Aunt Anna lives, one of their neighbors is taking his trash out. It's the same guy who was unfriendly to Aunt Anna the other day.

He doesn't seem to mind talking to my mom. "You her sister?" he asks when he sees us at Aunt Anna's door. "You look the same."

"Yes, we're sisters."

The man gives me the once over. "So you're his cousin?"

"Uh-huh." I don't feel like getting into a conversation with this guy.

"Good thing you're not autistic too," the man says as he walks off. His voice drops when he says the word *autistic*, as if he's afraid that by saying it too loud, he might catch it.

Mom's back stiffens. "You shouldn't talk that way about my nephew—or about anyone else," she says, but the guy is out of earshot.

Mom rings, but no one answers. The door is unlocked, so we walk in. Todd is sitting on the living room rug, hunched over the latest issue of *Aviation Week*.

"Todd, honey, we're here," Mom says.

Todd is muttering to himself, probably reading from the magazine.

Mom goes over to him. "I know this must be very stressful for you, Todd," she says.

This time, Todd grunts.

Because anything beats hanging out with Todd, I follow Mom into Aunt Anna and Uncle Fred's bedroom. The curtains are drawn and the lights are off. Aunt Anna is perched on the edge of the bed. Uncle Fred is lying down, though it's hard to know for sure it's him because the sheets are pulled over his head. The room smells like old gym socks.

Mom flicks on the light switch.

"No!" Uncle Fred moans from underneath the sheets.

Mom turns off the light.

"Has he eaten?" Mom asks Aunt Anna.

"Not a thing."

Mom walks over to the side of the bed. "Fred," she says, addressing the sheets, "you've got to see a doctor. We're worried about you."

Uncle Fred doesn't say anything. The sheets move up and down as he breathes.

"Fred," Mom continues, "Anna and I are going to take you to the hospital. We need you to get up now. Anna"—she pats my aunt's shoulder—"you'll need to pack him some clothes and his toothbrush."

"I'm not going," Uncle Fred says from underneath the sheets.

"Oh yes you are." I recognize my Mom's no-nonsense voice. I feel like telling Uncle Fred there's no point arguing with her. "If you don't go with us now, Jordie's going to phone an ambulance."

I am?

I can hear Aunt Anna rustling in the bathroom.

Mom kneels down. She whispers—I guess she doesn't want Aunt Anna to hear—"Fred, if they have to drag you out of here in an ambulance, it's going to be hard on Todd. It's a lot easier on him if you come with us now."

At first, Uncle Fred does not respond. But then he throws off the sheet that is covering his head and says, "All right. I'll go."

Aunt Anna is watching from the doorway. "Thank god," she says.

Mom helps Uncle Fred up. She even has to help him lace his shoes.

"What do you want me to do?" I ask her.

"You can look after Todd. We're taking Uncle Fred to emergency at Montreal General. If it's a long wait, you may be here all night, Jordie."

"You're kidding."

I try to distract Todd when Mom and Aunt Anna lead Uncle Fred out of the apartment. "Wanna show me that magazine?" I ask him. "Any Dash 8s in there?"

But my strategy fails. Todd lumbers over to the door, clutching the magazine under his arm. "Where's Dad going?" he wants to know.

This could be the first time I've ever heard Todd start a conversation that wasn't about airplanes. Todd is worried—the way any kid would worry about his dad.

Uncle Fred looks confused, and Mom and Aunt Anna are too busy steering Uncle Fred out the door to answer Todd. I figure it's up to me. "Your dad has to see the doctor. We're going to hang out."

"Hang out?"

"Yeah, me and you. Do stuff. Like cousins do," I tell him.

"Okay, we're going to hang out. Like cousins." Todd's voice is flat, but I get the feeling he's pleased.

I remember what Mom said in the van—how I'm only interested in my own well-being. So I try to think about Todd's well-being. About what would make him feel better right now. "Wanna show me your magazine collection?"

Todd keeps his magazines underneath his desk. "I have fifty-seven issues," he says. "Two are doubles. So it's really fifty-six."

I grab a magazine from the pile and start flipping through it.

Todd scratches under his arms. He keeps scratching. I know it's that stimming thing he does. Part of me wants to tell him to stop, but the nicer part of me knows I shouldn't.

I remember something Mom once told me: neurotypical people—that's the scientific term for people who do not have disorders like autism—engage in repetitive behaviors too.

"Ever notice how your dad is always playing with the remote?" she had asked me. Dad must have heard us talking because he called out from the other room, "Or how your mom is always pinching dead leaves off plants?"

Now Todd is straightening out the pile of magazines.

"All I did was grab the one on top," I tell him.

Todd looks down at the floor. "I like the edges lined up," he says.

"Why?"

Todd doesn't have an answer. Now that he's got the edges of his magazines lined up, he starts scratching at his pits again.

I need to do something to distract him. "I guess you're looking forward to visiting that flight school."

"Yeah."

Well, I think, that wasn't exactly a conversation starter. I need to come up with something better. "How many seats in a Dash 8?"

"The Dash 8-300 or the Dash 8-100?" Todd actually looks at me for a second.

"Uh, both, I guess."

"The Dash 8-300 has fifty seats. The 100 has thirty-seven seats. I also know their cruising altitudes."

"You do?" I try to sound interested.

"The Dash 8-300 and the Dash 8-100 have the same cruising altitude: twenty-five thousand feet."

"I'm sorry about your dad."

Todd's Adam's apple jiggles in his throat. Is it possible I am about to have a normal conversation with Todd, the kind of conversation regular cousins have? Is Todd going to say he's worried about his dad? And when he does, will I be able to say something helpful?

But when Todd speaks again, he doesn't mention Uncle Fred. "Twenty-five thousand feet," he says, "is seven thousand, six hundred and twenty meters."

Maybe Todd catches me looking at him funny. Or maybe he's worried about his dad. Because now Todd keeps repeating, "Twenty-five thousand feet is seven thousand, six hundred and twenty meters." He says it over and over, faster and faster like a top spinning round. "Twenty-five thousand feet is seven thousand, six…"

Todd pays no attention when I ask him quietly to stop.

In the end, I have no choice but to shout. "Stop it! Stop it now! You're driving me crazy!"

Todd stops.

Then he does something even worse.

He starts to cry. I've never seen anyone sob so hard.

Watching him is awful.

"Your dad's going to be okay," I tell him. "He's just going through a hard time."

Todd wipes the snot from his nose with the back of his hand.

"Don't hug me," he says when he finally calms down.

Chapter Twelve

I wonder if Aunt Anna had anything to do with choosing the destination for this field trip. She meets a lot with Mr. Delisle, so maybe it was her idea that the grade eights and nines visit a flight school. She must have known it would make Todd happy.

We take a bus to the school, which is in Lachute, a town in the foothills of the Laurentian Mountains. Todd and Darlene sit up front. But even from the back, where I sit with Tyrone, Mark and the girls, I can see Todd stimming. I don't know if it's because he's anxious (Uncle Fred has been in the hospital for over a week), or if he's excited about spending a day around airplanes.

"Do a lot of girls take flying lessons?" Isobel asks Mr. Gendron, the owner of the flying school and our tour guide for the day.

"More than half our clients are men," Mr. Gendron tells her, "but women make excellent pilots. Are you thinking of becoming a pilot?"

"Now I am!" Isobel says.

"Have you ever seen a crash?" Mark wants to know.

"Never," Mr. Gendron says. "We have a perfect safety record. When a plane crashes, it makes the news. But there are far more car accidents than plane crashes."

Our tour begins in a two-story office building. There's a snack bar on the main floor. Everyone laughs when Tyrone asks the woman standing behind the counter if she serves airplane food. "You know the kind that comes in plastic trays with foil wrapping?"

Mr. Gendron takes us upstairs to show us two classrooms and the dispatch office. That's where students book flights and pick up documents and keys.

"Every plane has its own logbook," Mr. Gendron says as he pulls out a logbook from the shelf and opens it. "Pilots and student pilots record their information after every flight. We also record all maintenance and service to the aircrafts."

Most kids wander down the hallway to look through the giant windows into the hangar, but not Todd. He's studying the logbook the way I would study for one of Mr. Dartoni's quizzes.

Darlene is standing by the wall, supervising from there.

I tense up when I see Mr. Gendron clap Todd on the shoulder. But Todd doesn't freak out. Maybe he is too absorbed in the logbook to notice. "You seem to be an extremely focused young man," Mr. Gendron tells Todd. "Maybe you should consider a career in aviation."

Todd doesn't react. But Darlene grins. "Oh, wouldn't that be wonderful?" she says.

The coolest thing upstairs is the flight simulator. Mr. Gendron explains how this machine—it's basically an armchair with a giant panel in front— teaches pilots how to fly in complete darkness. "See that part of the screen?" he says, pointing to a blacked-out area on the screen. That's what zero visibility looks like."

"I'd freak out," Samantha says.

"Not if you studied instrument flying," Mr. Gendron tells her. "Another thing I should explain is that pilots must constantly monitor weather conditions. You may have noticed the computer outside the dispatch office. Before every flight, our instructors and students check the weather. Weather is a tricky thing," he adds, gesturing to a window at the back of the room. "Today is a perfect example. It's bright and sunny, but by this afternoon, we're supposed to get record high winds. I can tell you that none of my planes will be in the air this afternoon. The good news for you people is that means you'll be able to visit one or two of the teaching planes on the ground."

"I really want to go inside a Cessna 172," Todd says.

Mr. Gendron looks impressed. "It's not often I meet someone your age who knows about airplanes."

I see a couple of kids nudge each other and I'm expecting someone— maybe Tyrone or Mark—to make a crack about Todd, but no one does.

When I hear a weird retching sound from the back of the room, my first thought is that someone must be airsick. My second thought is that doesn't make any sense since we aren't in the air.

Everyone else notices too. Darlene's hand is over her mouth and her eyes look like they might pop out of her head. It's clear to all of us that she is about to be sick.

"I think she needs a barf bag!" Tyrone calls out.

This time, no one laughs at Tyrone's joke.

Darlene rushes to the bathroom. When she comes out, she is so weak she can barely speak. She thinks it's food poisoning. Her husband is coming to get her. "Your mom is going to have to pick you up," she tells Todd, "or there won't be anyone to watch you."

When Todd's face crumbles, I know I have to do something.

"I'll watch out for Todd."

"You will?" Darlene and Tyrone say at the same time.

I can feel Samantha's eyes on my face.

I take a deep breath, and then I say, "I will." I pause for a second. Then I force myself to look right at Tyrone. "Look," I say, "there's something I never told you. Todd's my cousin."

Tyrone's mouth falls open. "No way," he says.

Mr. Gendron brings Darlene downstairs. Samantha goes to get her a glass of water. Darlene takes small sips.

Darlene taps my arm when I pass her. "Are you sure you can manage?" she asks.

"Sure I'm sure." I hope I sound more confident that I feel.

Chapter Thirteen

"He's your cousin?" Tyrone says. We've been inside the Cessna 172 (we took turns sitting in the pilot's seat). Now Mr. Gendron has gone back inside, and a few of us are walking along a runway. The wind is so strong we have to keep our faces down.

Mark nudges Tyrone. "I can't believe

you didn't figure that one out. Couldn't you tell from the hair?"

Todd is behind me.

"Yup," I say, "we're cousins." I try to make it sound like it's no big deal.

"How come you never said anything?" Tyrone asks me.

"Just because."

A brochure Isobel picked up at the dispatch office flies out of her hand. Tyrone tries catching it, but the wind sweeps up the brochure and sends it hurtling down the runway.

This sure is some crazy wind. It's whipping at our coats and howling in our ears. Another giant gust and the runway lights go out.

"Oh my god," Isobel squeals, "black out!"

We huddle closer. Tyrone puts his arm around Isobel.

Suddenly, there's a loud crack,

and a long thick branch comes flying at us. "Watch out!" Tyrone yells. Only it's too late. The branch whacks the side of Samantha's face.

"Are you okay?"

She can't hear me over the wind.

Samantha isn't okay. The right side of her face is already swollen. Now I make out an ugly gash on her cheek. It's bleeding. Samantha touches her cheek. She moans when she feels the blood.

I take off one of my mitts. Samantha winces when I press it against her face to stop the bleeding. "We need to get her back to the main building," I tell the others.

Only the wind is pushing us in the opposite direction.

"Who's got a cell?" Isobel has to shout so we can hear her.

Tyrone whips out his cell. He looks at the screen and then shakes the phone.

"Stupid thing isn't working. Maybe the wind blew out the cell tower."

"We can't just stand here," I say.

"Where are we supposed to go?" Tyrone shouts.

"We can go in there," Todd says.

We all turn to look at him. The others are as surprised as I am that Todd has said something.

"Go in where?" Tyrone asks Todd.

Todd gestures toward an airplane parked in front of us on the runway. "In there."

"It'll be locked," Tyrone says.

Todd shakes his head. "If there's a crash, people need to be able to open the doors from outside."

The little plane is only a couple of hundred feet away, but because of the wind, it takes us a while to reach it. Todd's right about the doors. They aren't locked. We pile inside.

Isobel finds a first-aid kit. There's antibiotic cream and gauze inside.

Samantha grimaces when Isobel applies the cream.

I'm the one who notices the blood in Samantha's right eye. Then Isobel sees it too. "Oh my god, Sam," she says. "Your eye—it's bleeding!"

"We need to get her to a doctor," I say.

"What are you planning to do—phone nine-one-one?" Tyrone asks. "'Cause there's no cell service."

"Does it hurt?" Isobel asks Samantha.

"Not really." Samantha squeezes her right eye shut and then opens it again. "I can't see from that eye," she says quietly.

Which is when Isobel starts screaming.

Todd tenses up. I can't blame him. The piercing sound of Isobel's scream fills the small plane.

Now Todd presses his hands over his ears and starts making this awful sound I've never heard before. It's like a horse whinnying. If it was anybody else, I'd put my hand on his shoulder to calm him down. But I can't touch Todd.

At least this makes Isobel stop screaming.

"Todd," I say as calmly as I can, "Isobel didn't mean to scare you. She's worried. Samantha needs a doctor, and the phone's not working." I can feel the others watching us. "Let's take a few deep breaths." I've seen Aunt Anna do this with Todd.

Todd and I breathe in and out. We do it a few times.

Todd drops his hands back to his sides and sighs. "If there's no phone," he says, "we can use the ELT."

"The ELT? What's an ELT?" I ask him.

"The emergency locator transmitter," Todd says. "Every plane has one. On a small plane like this it's usually in the cargo compartment."

The ELT is exactly where Todd said it would be. "Have you ever used one of these before?" Tyrone asks Todd.

"No," Todd says, "but I've read about them. An ELT gets activated automatically during a crash. There's a manual option too."

Ten minutes later, Mr. Gendron pulls up in the aviation-school truck. By the time we get to the hangar, the ambulance is already waiting for Samantha.

Chapter Fourteen

Todd sleeps over. Mom is impressed when I offer to sleep on the couch so he can have my bed. "He's a hero," I say, shrugging my shoulders.

"Thank goodness he knew about that ELT," Mom says.

"I'm a hero," Todd says when I go upstairs for a pillow.

"That's for sure," I tell him.

Todd talks to himself before he falls asleep. Even from the living room, I hear him repeating over and over, "I'm a hero. That's for sure." I think about going upstairs and complaining. But it probably wouldn't help. So I put the pillow over my head and fall asleep.

Aunt Anna has spent the night at the hospital with Uncle Fred. This morning, he is being transferred to the psychiatric ward. "It's the best place for him now," Mom explains over breakfast.

Todd observes his Wheaties floating in the milk.

"We'll drop by the hospital this morning. Does that sound okay, Todd?" Mom asks.

"Okay," Todd says without looking up.

Todd and I wait outside the gift shop when Mom goes in to buy a magazine for Aunt Anna. Todd shifts from one foot to the other. He doesn't look at me when he speaks. "It's my fault Dad's sad. Because I have autism."

"That's the dumbest thing I've ever heard," I tell him.

We have to get buzzed into the psychiatric ward. Uncle Fred's room feels like a prison cell. Aunt Anna sits on the bed, holding Uncle Fred's hand. Uncle Fred is snoring lightly, but he stirs when we come in.

He opens his eyes and looks at Todd, but Uncle Fred is too tired—or maybe too drugged—to speak. His face is stubbly, and he's wearing a green hospital gown. I want my old uncle back, the one who calls me his favorite nephew. If it's hard for me, what must this be like for Todd?

When I turn my head, I'm not surprised to see that Todd is scratching under his arms.

If stimming worked for me, I'd do it right now too.

"Fred, did you hear that Todd's a hero?" Mom says this extra loud, as if she thinks that by raising her voice, Uncle Fred might snap out of his depression. "He helped get a girl medical attention. There was a windstorm. The kids were visiting an aviation school."

Uncle Fred tries propping himself up. In a voice not much louder than a whisper, he tells Todd, "I'm proud of you, son." And then, as if saying that has taken all the energy he had, Uncle Fred slumps back down.

Mom and Aunt Anna are talking in the hallway. "I'll need to prepare Todd," I hear Aunt Anna say.

At first, I think they're talking about how long Uncle Fred will be in the hospital, only then Mom adds, "You don't want him finding out from the newspaper."

They're not talking about Uncle Fred.

They're talking about the letter. Aunt Anna must have decided to go public with it after all.

Uncle Fred needs his rest, and Aunt Anna wants to go home to shower. Mom agrees to drop Todd and me at the Children's Hospital so we can visit Samantha. She'll pick us up after she's taken Aunt Anna home.

Aunt Anna and Todd sit in the back of the van. I feel sick to my stomach when Aunt Anna starts talking about the hate letter. Why couldn't she wait to do that until the two of them are alone? Then I realize maybe she wants Mom's support—and mine too.

"Todd, honey," Aunt Anna begins, "you know what your dad said—about being proud of you? I'm proud of you too. Not just for helping that girl, but for being you. Look, there's something important we need to discuss." She waits for Todd to respond, but when he doesn't, she continues. "Someone really ignorant wrote a cruel letter—a hateful letter—about you and about people with autism. I wasn't going to tell you, but I've changed my mind. Because you know what, Todd?" Aunt Anna's voice breaks, "You keep demonstrating how smart and brave you are. I think we need to go public with the letter. Not just for you. For other kids with autism."

Mom bites her lip. "Todd," she says as she watches him in the rearview mirror, "you need to tell your mom if you're not comfortable with this."

"Your Aunt Julie is right. Are you okay with me sending a copy of the letter to the newspaper?"

Todd doesn't say yes or no. He just repeats something Aunt Anna said before, "A hateful letter about people with autism."

Mom sucks in her breath. "I'm still not sure it's the right thing to do, Anna."

"It's a pretty bad letter," I say.

"How do you know?" Mom and Aunt Anna ask at the same time.

"I…uh…I saw it. On the computer."

"You were reading my email?" Mom asks.

"It just kinda happened. You really need a lesson about Internet safety."

"That's not what this is about, Jordie."

Aunt Anna interrupts. "If Jordie's read the letter, he'll be able to support Todd if it goes public."

"That's right. I will." I have to say that. It's the only way to end the argument.

Even with a patch over one eye, Samantha looks good. We find her sitting in the lounge at the Children's Hospital. Her dad is with her. "I've got a vitreous hemorrhage," Samantha says. "Sitting up helps the blood vessels drain to the bottom of my eye. The good news is I'm not blind."

"Phew," I say.

Maybe it's because of the patch that Samantha doesn't notice right away that Todd's behind me.

"Todd!" she says when she sees him. She starts getting up from her chair, but her dad stops her.

"Samantha! The doctor said absolutely no bouncing around for at least twenty-four hours! Are you Todd?"

Samantha doesn't listen to her dad. She goes over to Todd—and kisses him.

Todd squirms and then wipes at his cheek. Not surprisingly, he's stimming again.

I sure wish Samantha would kiss me like that. I wonder if Samantha knows what I'm thinking—because I get the feeling she's trying not to laugh. "Hey, Jordie," she says, "I need to thank you too."

"Thank me? For what?"

"For having such a cool cousin."

Samantha's dad reaches out to shake Todd's hand, but I stop him. "Todd doesn't like when people touch him. Especially people he's not used to."

"I see," Samantha's dad says. "Well, young man, we're very grateful for what you did."

A woman with blond spiky hair is walking toward us. I'm almost sure it's the woman I heard bad-mouthing kids like Todd at parent-teacher night.

"Are you guys having a party without me?" Now I recognize the nasal voice.

"Todd, Jordie," Samantha says, "I don't think you've met my stepmom."

"Oh my god," Samantha's stepmom puts her hand over her mouth when she sees Todd. "You're the kid who saved Samantha? I didn't realize it was you."

Chapter Fifteen

We're having a family meeting at Aunt Anna's. We ordered in cheese pizza— it's the only kind Todd likes. Mom and I are sitting on one side of the table. Aunt Anna and Todd are across from us.

Aunt Anna's hands shake when she starts talking about the letter. "I don't think you need to read it, honey," she tells Todd. Her eyes are already filled with tears.

"I don't need to read it," Todd says.

"But I think you need to understand a little more," Aunt Anna continues. "About the sorts of things that are in it."

Mom shakes her head. Aunt Anna leans closer to Todd. I'm facing him. This is going to be torture.

"The person who wrote it doesn't know anything about autism," Aunt Anna says. "The letter is full of misconceptions and prejudice. It says people with autism are...that they..." Aunt Anna is getting really choked up now.

Mom reaches across the table to pat Aunt Anna's hand.

Todd swallows a couple of times. He scratches under his armpits, but only once. "Some people think I'm a freak," he says. His voice is flat, but his lower lip is trembling.

I can't take much more of this. "Maybe we shouldn't focus on the letter," I say quietly. "Maybe we should focus on a plan of action instead. A plan Todd's okay with."

"I just want to be sure that Todd understands," Mom says. "Like your mom said," she adds, looking at Todd, "the letter is full of misconceptions and prejudice. There are people who don't know much about autism. And people are afraid of what they don't know. So they lash out by saying—or writing—cruel things."

"I'm not a freak," Todd whispers.

"Of course you're not," I tell him.

"But someone wrote that," Todd says.

Mom's eyes flash. "Someone ignorant and cruel wrote that," she says.

"Someone cowardly," Aunt Anna adds. "That's why they didn't sign their name."

Todd does something unusual now: he looks at me. I can tell he expects me to say something.

"I don't think you're a freak." And because I don't know what else to say,

I add, "Samantha definitely doesn't think so."

Todd thinks about that for a minute. "I helped save Samantha," he says. "Samantha understands about autism. A lot of people don't."

"You're right," Aunt Anna says. "That's why I want to tell the newspaper about this hate mail."

"Okay," Todd says. "Tell the newspaper."

The story makes the front page of *The Gazette*. There's a picture of Aunt Anna holding the letter. Todd is in the picture too, but he's in the background, reading one of his aviation magazines, and his face is fuzzy. The hate letter is on page three of the paper.

None of us expected that the article—and the letter—would go viral. By the time I get home from school the day after the article was in the paper, it's all over Facebook and Twitter. There are a couple of nasty comments, but most are sympathetic. "What can we do to help Todd and kids like him?" one of them asks.

Uncle Fred has been complaining about the hospital food, so Todd and I bring him a cheeseburger and fries. The nurse who's giving Uncle Fred his pills smiles when she sees Todd. "I noticed the last name on your dad's chart," she says. "You're Todd, right?"

Todd is looking at the floor. "I guess you read the article."

"I saw it on Facebook. It's an honor to meet you," the nurse says. "You're a brave guy."

"He takes after his old man," Uncle Fred says.

It's the first joke Uncle Fred has made in nearly three weeks. I decide it's a sign that he's going to make a full recovery.

Chapter Sixteen

"I think Samantha's hot," Todd says.

"Hotter than a Dash 8?" I ask.

We are sitting at the donut shop where Samantha works. She sent me a text asking us to meet her here. The air smells sweet and lemony, and I now understand why Samantha always smells so delicious. Her good smell isn't perfume, it's donuts.

Samantha is behind the counter, serving customers. Todd and I munch on our lemon-filled donuts while we wait for her to get her break.

A guy in a long wool coat walks by and taps his knuckles on our table. Todd bristles. It's that weird guy who lives on his floor. "You know what I heard?" the man says. He sure doesn't have very good social skills.

"Uh, hello." I hope that'll give him the message.

It doesn't.

"I heard some people say that letter is a hoax. They said you people made it up to get attention. But I told them you wouldn't do that. I said I was sure it was a real letter."

"It's a real letter," Todd says.

Before he shuffles off to his own table, the man looks back at Todd and says, "Listen, kid, I'm sorry if I've been unfriendly. I guess I didn't know much about autism."

Samantha catches the end of the conversation. "Hey," she says to the man, "there's gonna be a rally on Saturday morning to raise awareness about autism. We're meeting in front of Riverview High School at ten. You should totally come!"

The man can't resist Samantha's charm any more than Todd or I can. "Ten?" he says. Then he reaches into his pocket, takes out his agenda and a small pencil, and makes a note about the rally.

Todd is shredding his napkin into tiny pieces. I bet he's nervous about the rally. There could be a lot of new people there, and they might get closer to him than he's comfortable with.

"How does it feel to be a hero?" Samantha asks him when she sits down.

"Good. I guess."

"I was thinking," I say to both of them, "maybe Todd won't like being right in the middle of the rally. Maybe we can find a way for him to participate—but still give him his space."

Todd has made a neat pile out of the bits of shredded napkin. "I like to have my space," he says.

"Well then, we'll make sure you get plenty of space," Samantha tells Todd.

That is when I realize Samantha is not just being nice—she really likes Todd and appreciates his quirkiness. I should be happy for Todd, but instead I feel jealous. "So, do you get to eat all the donuts you want?" I ask Samantha, hoping to get her attention back on me.

"To be honest, I'm sick of donuts." Samantha has a pink scar on her cheek where the branch hit her, but her eye looks normal.

"So what'd you want to talk to us about?" I ask her.

"I got you guys something," Samantha says.

"Is it donuts?" Todd asks.

When Samantha cracks up, I start feeling jealous again. "It's way better than donuts. Close your eyes, okay? Both of you."

We close our eyes. I can hear Samantha running to the back of the donut shop. When she comes back, she is out of breath. "Okay," she says, "you can open your eyes."

Samantha hands me and Todd a beautifully wrapped package. "It's something you can work on together," she says.

Todd and I tear off the wrapping. Samantha has bought us a kit to build a model Cessna 172. "Wow," I say, "what a great present. It's got four hundred pieces. And it comes with a pilot and four passengers." I know it's Samantha's way of telling us she'll never forget that day at the flight school.

Todd is inspecting the box.

"Do you like it?" Samantha asks him.

Todd puts the box down and starts rearranging the napkin bits. "The Cessna 172 is okay. But the Dash 8 is still my favorite," he says.

I figure any minute now Samantha is going to run out of patience with Todd and realize I am a far better guy for her than my cousin.

But Samantha is not upset. "You know what I like best about you, Todd?" she asks.

Now Todd is scratching his pits.

"I like your honesty." Samantha reaches across the table. For a second, I think she is going to take Todd's hand, but instead she reaches for the model kit. "How 'bout on Saturday, after the rally, we go to the hobby store and see if we can exchange this for a Dash 8 kit?"

As if things weren't bad enough, now Todd and Samantha are going to be hanging out together after the rally.

I am trying to think of how I can fix things. Only I don't have to. Because Todd has a question.

"Can Jordie come too?" he wants to know.

Chapter Seventeen

It's too bad Uncle Fred can't be at the rally. At least he's sleeping and eating again. Mom thinks it's a combination of the new meds and his sessions with the psychiatrist. It turns out the psychiatrist is a documentary-film buff—so I guess she and Uncle Fred have lots to talk about.

A crowd has formed in the school-yard. Many people are carrying placards that say things like *Down With Hate Mail* and *Autism Is Not a Disease— Ignorance Is*.

As I'm stepping out of the van, Todd hands me a folded-up piece of paper, which I slip into my pocket. "You sure?" I ask him.

"Uh-huh," he says.

Now I notice the banner over the front entrance of the school. *Todd's Our Hero*.

Todd is going to stay in the van with Mom, Dad and Aunt Anna. Dad has unrolled the windows so Todd can be part of the rally and apart from it at the same time. I catch Dad's eye and point to the banner, so he'll be sure Todd sees it too.

A few kids who spot Todd through the open window start chanting his name. *Todd! Todd! Todd!*

When I look back at Todd, I see he's got his hands over his ears.

"Hey," I call out to the crowd in my loudest voice. "No chanting, okay?"

Mr. Delisle comes over to where I am standing. That must be his wife with him. I hope no one mentions what he said at the assembly about his mother-in-law!

Mr. Delisle addresses the crowd. "Ladies and gentlemen, boys and girls," he says, "now that Todd and his family have arrived, this rally can officially begin. Our guest of honor prefers to be part of the procession from inside the van. The rest of us are going to be walking to city hall to raise awareness about autism."

Teachers, kids and even the guy from Todd's building have come out for the rally.

I give Todd a thumbs-up before I join the crowd.

For a second, Todd looks puzzled, but then he gives me a thumbs-up back.

Darlene is there too. She's walking with a group of Riverside teachers.

Dad is driving the van slowly to the right of the crowd. When the van stops for a light, some kids start pressing in on it. They want to see Todd—and talk to him. "One at a time," I call out.

Tyrone apologizes for what happened at the Halloween dance. Mark is going to Florida at Christmas, and he wants to know what Todd thinks of Air Canada's Boeing 767.

"The 767-300 ER?" Todd asks.

"Uh, I guess," Mark says.

"The 767-300 ER was Boeing's first wide-body twinjet," Todd says.

Mark whistles.

At the next light, Mark's sister wants to meet Todd. She's reaching into the van, when I stop her. "Todd doesn't like when people he doesn't know get too close," I explain.

Samantha pushes her way through the crowd to join me. "Can you believe all these people?" she says. "And they're all here for Todd!"

As we approach city hall, Mr. Delisle and his wife come to march next to us. "Jordie," Mr. Delisle says, "I'm going to say a few words when we get there. I understand you've agreed to say something too."

"Yup," I say. "That's the plan."

Mr. Delisle explains a little about autism and how there are more and more students with autism in the public school system. Then he tells everyone about what happened at the flight school and how Todd was a hero. Mr. Delisle also gives his speech about acceptance.

Then it's my turn.

"I just want to say thanks to all of you for turning up today to show your support."

When I realize I've been talking to my feet, I look up. That's when I notice a blond-haired woman walking over to join the crowd. Samantha's stepmom.

I reach into my pocket. "Todd wrote a letter he wants me to read for him."

The crowd gets so quiet I can hear the sound of people around me breathing. I unfold the letter. In a weird way, I feel like Todd when I start reading it. As if we're one person. "Hello," the letter begins.

"A lot of things are hard for people like me who have autism. Such as making eye contact and hearing loud noises and being part of a crowd. That's why I asked my cousin Jordie to read this letter for me.

"I heard about the hate mail. A lot of people want to know who wrote it. But not me. Because, in a way, that letter did something good. It let me find out that you think I'm okay. That you don't think I'm a freak."

My voice breaks a little when I read that part.

"I want to say thank you to all of you for coming out today. I also want you to know that people with autism can do anything we want to do. Even if it's hard for us. And if you really want to help people like me, this is what you can do. You can treat us like we're human beings. You can ask us to do stuff with you."

People are clapping now, but I can tell they're trying not to make too much noise—they're clapping gently.

I clear my throat to let the crowd know there's still another paragraph left in Todd's letter. "I want to say an extra thanks to my mom, my dad, Aunt Julie and Uncle Lou. And especially to my best friend"—I clear my throat again; I really hope no one knows how close I am to crying—"Jordie."

Acknowledgments

Hate Mail is the result of a project called *Libres comme l'art*. Made possible by the Blue Metropolis Literary Foundation, the Conférence régionale des élus de Montréal (CREM), and the Conseil des Arts de Montréal (CAM), *Libres comme l'art* allowed me to be writer-in-residence at Riverdale High School in Pierrefonds, Quebec, during the 2013–14 school year. Together with Karen Scott's grade-nine English class, we brainstormed ideas for this novel. The students heard almost every chapter as I was writing it. They laughed at the right spots and groaned or raised their hands when things needed fixing. I am grateful to Ms. Scott's students: Saba-Lou Ahmad Khan, Megan Amofa, Tyrelle Anasara-Diab, Shane Jermie Antoine, Hamzah Bashir Ahmad, Matthew Boucher, Ali Chaudhry,

Kelly Cooperberg, Mae-Ann Dilidili-Sales, Kayla D'Ovidio, Rupert Jr. Edwards, Christian Ehninger, Fahad Elsabawi, Alicia Frederick, Cassidy Freidman, Shayne Gallagher, Devontay Green, Sabrina Hilton-Cuillerier, Sarah Joly, Awaiz Junjua, Christopher Kelly, Darlens Leveque, Jared Logan, Liam-Marshall MacLellan, Bhahee Shan Manoranjan, Brett Marineau, Georgia Pournaras, Amanda Powell, Jordana Schmits, John Skalkogiannis, Vito Tarantino and Kiara West-Philippeaux. A special thanks to Hamzah, who, during our first session, mentioned a hate letter targeting an autistic child that had recently made the news. Special thanks also to Ms. Scott for sharing her students; to student teacher Christina Christopoulos; to Principal Roger Rampersad for his enthusiastic support; to librarian Susan Strano for opening up her library for the project;

and to Suzanne Nesbitt of the Lester B. Pearson School Board for bringing the project to Riverdale. I'm also grateful to the terrific team at Blue Metropolis, in particular its president, William St-Hilaire, for her wise and energetic leadership; Florence Allegrini, who got things started; and Laure Colin, who oversaw every step of the way. Thanks also to Frédérique Bélair-Bonnet of CREM and Réjane Bougé of CAM. Thanks to Craig Quinn for talking to me about airplanes, and to Philippe Gélinas for inviting me to visit Dorval Aviation School. Thanks also to my friend Elizabeth Arnot for reading an early draft and providing invaluable feedback. Finally, thanks to the super team at Orca, especially to my editor, Melanie Jeffs, for her astute and sensitive comments.

Monique Polak has written several books in the Orca Currents series, including *Pyro* and *121 Express*, an ALA Popular Paperbacks selection. Monique lives in Montreal, Quebec. For more information, visit www.moniquepolak.com.